Gordy and the Ghost Crab

Dedicated to Lillian and Oliver

Gordy and the Ghost Crab

Written and Illustrated by

Linda K. Sienkiewicz

Writer's Coffee Bar Press

New Jersey

Staying at the beach,
for a week had sounded cool,
but the sea wasn't tame
like a round swimming pool.

So Gordy stayed on the sand,
pretending to be brave,
playing far away from
the knock-you-down waves.

Then a crazy looking critter,
with a zillion legs or more,
skittered from the sea,
and up onto the shore.

Gordy tried to chase it,
but it vanished in thin air.
Or perhaps it scurried down
that hole right over there.

Or this one? Or that one?
There were so very many.
Some as large as golf balls,
others small as pennies.

He hollered down one hole,
"Hey you, come on out!"
and kicked sand at another,
"Didn't you hear me shout?"

His brother grinned and said,
"That's a ghost crab don't you know,
with pincers sharp enough
to snip off all your toes.

Then it drags them deep
into its sandy hole,
and eats them up
in a hot dog roll."

Gordy wasn't sure
about his brother's story,
but he backed away.
Better safe than sorry!

He tried not to ponder
that toe-snipping tale,
and returned to building castles
with his shovel and his pail.

Soon another ghost crab appeared by Gordy's side, waving pincers in the air and looking terrified.

A pony-tailed girl,
was racing 'cross the sand,
heading toward the two of them,
a net clasped in her hand!

"I'm a ghost crab hunter!"
She swung her fearsome net.
"And the next one that I catch,
I'll take home for a pet."

Gordy knew the little crab
wouldn't want to be
caught up in her net
and taken from the sea!

"No crabs here" he said,
and kicked his pail upside-down
to hide the little ghosty
from her super scary frown.

She squinted hard at Gordy, tapped one foot and glared. Then answered with a sigh, "Well, I never really cared."

Then Gordy raised the pail,
and let the crab run free.
It skittered toward the waves,
and headed straight to sea.

"Thanks for leaving me my toes,"
he called out with delight,
as his friend, the ghost crab,
slipped right out of sight.

Fun Facts About Ghost Crabs

WHY ARE THEY CALLED GHOST CRABS?

Most active at night, their pale bodies match the sand making them almost invisible. Some ghost crabs can change their color to blend with the sand throughout the day and into evening.

HOW BIG ARE GHOST CRABS?

With boxy looking bodies, most grow to about two inches wide, although you might find one as big as four inches. Instead of bones, they have a hard outer shell or exoskeleton. Ghost crabs breathe through gills like a fish, and must periodically wet them with seawater, but they can't swim or stay underwater for very long.

WHERE DO GHOST CRABS LIVE?

They live in burrows that they dig on sandy shores. Their homes may be as deep as four feet!

WHAT DO GHOST CRABS EAT?

Ghost crabs are scavengers who will eat just about anything they find on the beach. Their favorite foods are turtle eggs and hatchlings, bugs, snails, clams, mole crabs and sea plants.

HOW FAST ARE GHOST CRABS?

They are fast runners and take off at the first sign of danger. They can dart forwards, backwards, and sideways using all their legs at the same time.

DO GHOST CRABS MAKE NOISES?

A ghost crab talks by making a squeaky sound when it rubs the ridges on its right claw against its hairy leg. They also make thumping noises by pounding their pincers on the sand. One crab might say to another, "I want to be alone in my burrow," or "I like you. Be my friend."

MORE FUN FACTS ABOUT CRABS

A crab can use its claws in a lot of different ways: as a vice, scissors or a fork!

The Japanese Spider crab is the largest crab. They can grow as big as thirteen feet across.

Crabs are called spiders of the sea because their legs have joints just like spiders.

The smallest crab is the pea crab. How small is it? As small as a pea!

A crab's eyes are made up of hundreds of little lenses so they can see in all directions at the same time, even behind them!

Crabs have two front claws or pincers, and walk on four pairs of legs.

Hermit crabs help each other by trading shells to live in.

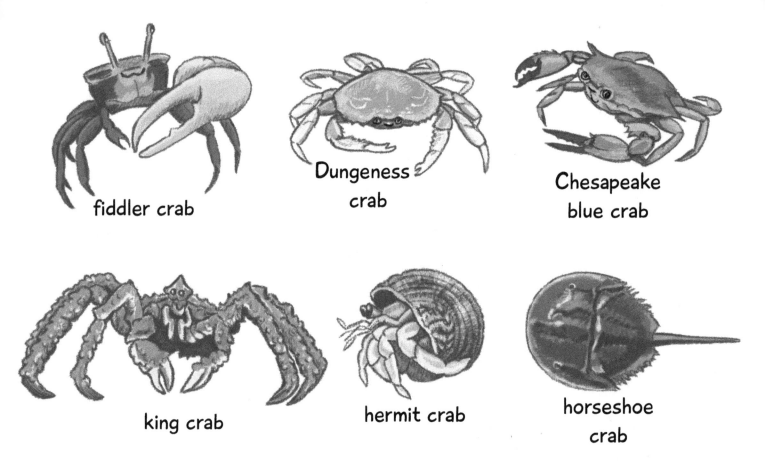

fiddler crab

Dungeness crab

Chesapeake blue crab

king crab

hermit crab

horseshoe crab

WHAT OTHER KINDS OF CRABS ARE THERE?

There are thousands of types of crabs! They live on the shores of beaches and coastal waterways, and in oceans all around the world.

Some of the best known are: fiddler, Dungeness, Cheasepeake blue, king, hermit and horseshoe crabs, but three of these are not true crabs. Can you guess which ones?

King, hermit and horseshoe are *not* true crabs.

Scientists can tell if human activity is disturbing beach life by surveying ghost crab burrows. A healthy beach will have lots of ghost crabs!

Ghost crabs are shy and don't like to be caught in nets or have their homes trampled on or destroyed by people, so please be careful. It's fun to look for ghost crabs at night with a flashlight, and then let them be on their way. They are fun to watch, but can't be kept as pets, so leave them at the beach and you can see them again on your next visit.

Oh, one last thing, a ghost crab won't pinch you . . .

unless you try to pick it up.

Cover and Book Layout/Design by MaryChris Bradley
ISBN 978-1-941523-22-3 (Paperback Original)
Library of Congress Control Number: 2020919869
First Paperback Edition, November 2020

CPSIA information can be obtained
at www.ICGtesting.com
Printed in the USA
BVHW020101241120
593324BV00007B/14